"Rematch!" story by Susan Amerikaner

Illustrated by Scott Tilley, Andrew Phillipson, Janelle Bell-Martin, Dan Gracey, Seung Beom Kim, and the Disney Storybook Art Team

For information address Disney Press, 1101 Flower Street, Glendale, California 91201.

Printed in the United States

First Edition

1 3 5 7 9 10 8 6 4 2

ISBN 978-1-4847-0473-8
G942-9090-6-13340

For more Disney Press fun, visit www.disneybooks.com

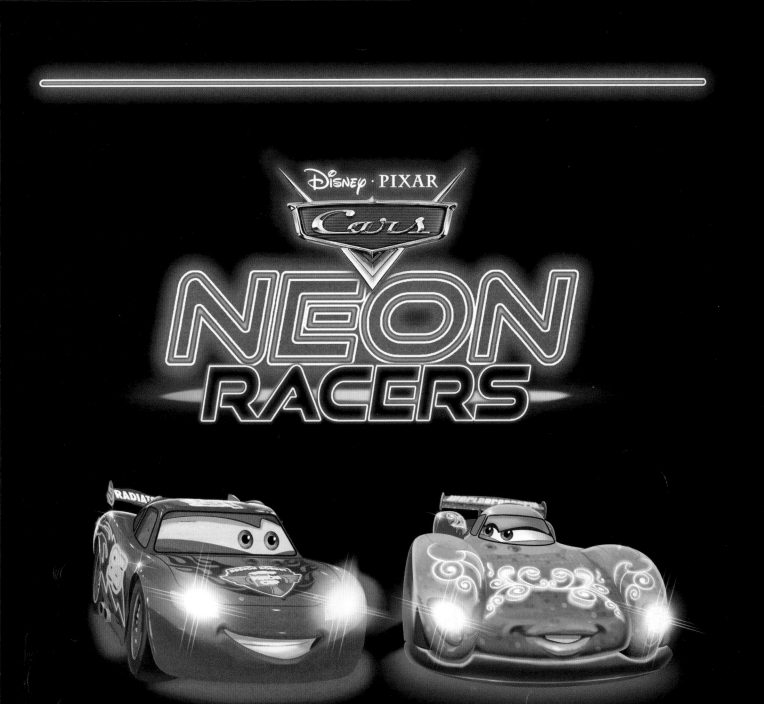

ightning McQueen was competing in the
Transcontinental Race of Champions—T-ROC—a
series of races hosted by his international racing friends. Now
Lightning was in Japan for a race hosted by Shu Todoroki.

"Buona sera, Lightning!" Francesco said. "Francesco is looking forward
to beating you in Tokyo again."

"Then I'm afraid Francesco will be very disappointed . . . especially
when he sees this." Lightning spun around and showed off a
"Sayonara Francesco!" bumper sticker.

You boys are so wrapped up in your own rivalry, you won't even notice when I speed right past you," said Carla Veloso with a wink.

Before Lightning or Francesco could respond, a white car cruised up to the racers. It was Mach Matsuo, Shu Todoroki's crew chief. "Welcome to Japan, everyone. Shu is waiting for you at our racing headquarters. If you'll follow me, I'll show you the way...."

At his headquarters, Shu explained the race. "We'll be racing at night—an 85-mile trip from Mount Fuji to Ginza."

Shu motioned for several of his pit crew members to come forward. "Since we'll be racing in the dark, we'll all need to be outfitted with special **competition lighting**." Shu darkened his race shop. The other racers gasped. **Shu was glowing!**

The next evening, the racers—all lit up in bright neon—met at Base Camp 5, halfway up Mount Fuji.

"Welcome, racers," said Shu. "When the flag drops, you may head straight down the mountain. But, for those who would like to join the ranks of Mount Fuji's most legendary racers, you may head up . . . and sign the climbers' book at the top of the mountain!"

The racers gazed up at the summit.

"That climb looks intense," said Rip. "You can count me out—it's straight to Ginza for me."

"Francesco agrees with Rip," said the Formula car. "Francesco will win the race and then sign autographs!"

"The choice is yours," said Shu. "Ganbatte minna-san! Good luck, everyone!"

スタートライン
START LINE

24

The flag dropped and **the racers took off!** Francesco and most of the other racers headed down the mountain. But Lightning wasn't about to take the easy way out. **He wanted the honor of signing the climbers' book!**

Lightning, Shu, Carla, Lewis, and Vitaly Petrov, the Russian racer, drove up the rugged terrain, hugging the curves and skidding across patches of ice on their way to the summit, **their neon lighting the way.**

日本7

When the racers reached the summit, Shu called out, "There it is! The climbers' book!"

"Ka-chow!" Lightning cried, signing the book. The other racers followed suit.

As the racers turned to head back down the mountain, Shu stopped them. "I forgot to mention the other reward for reaching the peak of Mount Fuji: there's another road that leads straight down! Follow me!"

"Now you're talkin'!" yelled Lightning.

The five racers flew down the mountain. As it became warmer, the snow grew thinner. At the bottom of the mountain, a breeze rustled cherry blossom trees, showering the racers with pink petals. Racing fans with thunder sticks were lined up all along the course, **creating as much noise as they could**.

Lightning, Shu, Carla, Lewis, and Vitaly continued past forests and golden temples. **Suddenly, their road merged with another**, and the racers spotted Max, Frosty, Rip, and Nigel just ahead of them. They had caught up with the other racers!

"Let's show them what neon speed really looks like!" yelled Lightning.

The racers sped up, **their lights glowing brightly**. They looked like streaks of red, gold, green, and blue in the night.

Soon, Lightning caught up to Francesco.

"Lightning McQueen! Where did you come from?" asked Francesco in shock.

"You didn't think I'd make this easy on you, did you, Francesco?" asked Lightning. Smiling and **revving his engine**, he took the lead!

Finally, the racers entered Tokyo's colorful Ginza District. There were fans everywhere—screaming and waving the flags of their favorite racers. As the cars neared the finish line, Francesco edged out a lead. But with a burst of speed, Lightning cut in front of him! The two racers were so focused on passing each other, they didn't notice a car behind them. It was Carla Veloso! As promised, she slipped by the two competitors and won the race!

On the winner's podium, Shu presented Carla with the **Neon Racers Cup trophy**.

"Neon racing was amazing! Thanks for hosting, Shu," said Lightning. Then he turned to his friends. **"So . . . where to next?"**

Lightning McQueen and Francesco Bernoulli had challenged each other to a race in Monza, Italy—Francesco's hometown.

"Benvenuto!" said Francesco. "Your plane was late, but this is no surprise. **You will be late crossing the finish line, too.**"

Lightning smiled. Then he whispered to Mater, "I am so beating him—right here on his own turf!"

As the racers left the airport, they were surrounded by photographers.

"Everyone loves Francesco. He has many fans," said Francesco.

"Nobody has more fans than Lightning!" Mater piped up.

Francesco rolled his eyes.

"We will prove it!" said Luigi. "Lightning gets hundreds of fan letters each day. **Guido, bring the mailbags!**"

Guido zoomed off!

Guido returned with mailbags overflowing with fan letters.

Lightning was a little embarrassed. "Oh, it's really not that big of a deal," he said.

"You are right, Lightning," said Francesco. **"It is no big deal because Francesco has much, much more fan mail!"**

"Letters are great," said Lightning. "But we like to get some fender-to-fender time with our fans whenever we can."

As Lightning greeted all the cars who were lined up to see him, Mater really got the fans going. They began chanting: **"Light-NING! Light-NING!"**

"Questo è ridicolo!" mumbled Francesco. **"And what about autographs?"** he asked. "Watch—and be amazed."

Francesco started spinning his wheels and spewing out hundreds of autographed photos of himself to his fans. "See? Francesco always gets things done at **three hundred kilometers an hour**."

After the two racers finished greeting their fans, they drove to a café.

"Hey, Mr. Francesco, nobody drinks oil faster than Lightning," said Mater.

"What?" said Lightning. "Mater, I can't drink . . ."

"C'mon buddy, show 'em what I done taught you!" said Mater.

Lightning sighed and managed to finish a can of oil in a few gulps.

Francesco was not impressed. "Francesco never guzzles," he said. **"Oil should be savored."**

Lightning cruised over to Francesco. "How about a warm-up before the big race—just you and me?" he asked.

Francesco nodded. *"Ah, good idea, Lightning! Try to keep up, if you . . ."*

Before Francesco could finish, Lightning was a red streak down the road!

"Ka-*ciao*, Francesco!" yelled Lightning.

Francesco had almost caught up with Lightning when he nearly spun out on a left turn.

"How do you make those left turns so well?" Francesco asked Lightning.

"Get equipped with some treaded tires," said Lightning. "Then **turn right to go left**. A very good friend taught me that once."

Soon, the race cars stopped to rest.

Francesco sighed. **"Ahh, Italia is beautiful, no? Just like Francesco!"**

Lightning chuckled. "Do you always think about yourself?" he asked.

"Of course," said Francesco. "On the racetrack, Francesco only thinks about himself and doing his best. **This is why he always wins!**"

The next day was the big race. Finally, the v
who was the fastest race car! When the
went wild!

Francesco came out of the first left t
showed off his new treaded tires. **"
taught Francesco too well!"**

Lightning couldn't help but smile.

The racers entered the Monza arena and made a pit stop. As Lightning zoomed out of the pits, he got distracted by the camera flashes and the screaming fans. Suddenly, Lightning remembered what Francesco had said about focusing on himself and doing his best. **Lightning looked straight ahead and took the lead!**

CAR BONARA

As the two cars crossed the finish line, the crowd gasped.

"Ka-chow!" yelled Lightning. **"I won!"**

"You mean ciao bella," said Francesco. **"Francesco won!"**

The truth stunned everyone. According to the judges, the race was a ... **TIE!!!**

The cars tried to figure out what to do.

Then Francesco shouted, "No more talk! Talk is slow. What do we do? **We race!**"

"That's a great idea!" said Lightning. **"We'll race in Radiator Springs!"**

Then the two fastest cars in the world zoomed away together . . . to race again another day.

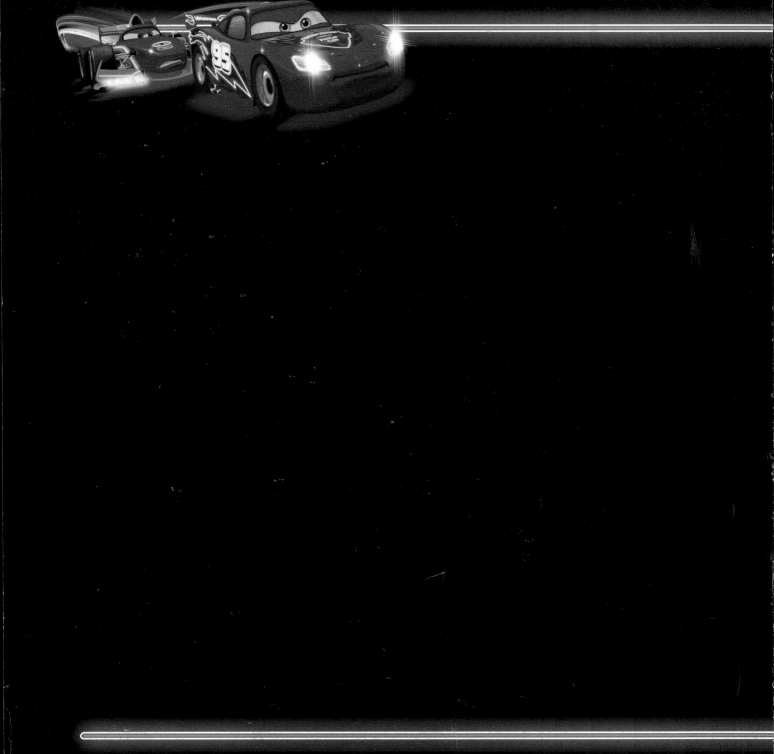